Sparkly New Friends

Read more UNICORN and YETI books!

UNICORN and YETI

Sparkly New Friends

written by
Heather Ayris Burnell

art by
Hazel Quintanilla

ACORN™
SCHOLASTIC INC.

For Ellamae, who has always been an amazing friend — HAB

To my brother and sister, my Yeti and Unicorn from real life — HQ

Text copyright © 2019 by Heather Ayris Burnell
Illustrations copyright © 2019 by Hazel Quintanilla

Library of Congress Cataloging-in-Publication Data

Names: Burnell, Heather Ayris, author. | Quintanilla, Hazel, 1982- illustrator.
Title: Sparkly new friends / by Heather Ayris Burnell ; illustrated by Hazel Quintanilla.
Description: First edition. | New York, NY : Acorn/Scholastic Inc., 2019. |
Series: Unicorn and Yeti ; 1 | Summary: Unicorn and Yeti run into each
other (literally) while looking for sparkly things, and despite some
differences, (for instance Unicorn is magic, Yeti is not, Yeti likes
snowball fights, Unicorn cannot throw snowballs)—the two become friends.
Identifiers: LCCN 2018035380 | ISBN 9781338329018 (pbk.) | ISBN 9781338329025 (hardcover)
Subjects: LCSH: Unicorns—Juvenile fiction. | Yeti—Juvenile fiction. |
Friendship--Juvenile fiction. | Humorous stories. | CYAC:
Unicorns—Fiction. | Yeti—Fiction. | Friendship—Fiction. | Humorous
stories. | LCGFT: Humorous fiction.
Classification: LCC PZ7.B92855 Sp 2019 | DDC [E]—dc23 LC record available at http://catalog.loc.gov

10 9 8 7 6 5 4 3 2 1   19 20 21 22 23

Printed in China   62

First edition, May 2019

Edited by Katie Carella
Book design by Sarah Dvojack

Table of Contents

Something Sparkly

Unicorn saw something sparkly.

Wow!

Yeti saw something sparkly.

3

You live in the most sparkly place I have ever seen!

There are no sparkles where I live. It is white here.

There are **lots** of sparkles here!

10

11

You are trying to trick me,
because you are so sparkly.

You are a tricky, sparkly horse
with a horn on your head.

13

No. I will not leave.

We will leave!

Come on. I will show you the sparkles.

Unicorn and Yeti flew up . . .

and up . . .

and down.

But mostly up.

The sun is very bright up here.

Look down!

22

An Amazing Friend

Unicorn, why do you have a horn on your head?

I do not know. I was just born this way.

Lots of things.

You are an amazing friend. I would like you even if you could not do magic.

I know. You did not know I could do magic until I just showed you. And we were already friends.

Friends don't need magic to like each other.

No, they do not!

35

37

Snowball Fight

Splat!

Did you **throw** that at me?
I thought we were friends.

It was just a snowball.

Throwing things at your friends
is not nice.

But throwing snowballs is fun.

43

First you make a big pile of snowballs.

Making snowballs is hard.

Next you build a fort to protect yourself.

Building a fort is hard.

46

Maybe throwing snowballs is not so easy when you have hooves instead of hands.

It is not easy.

I still think you can do it. Want to try again?

Splat!

I've been hit!

55

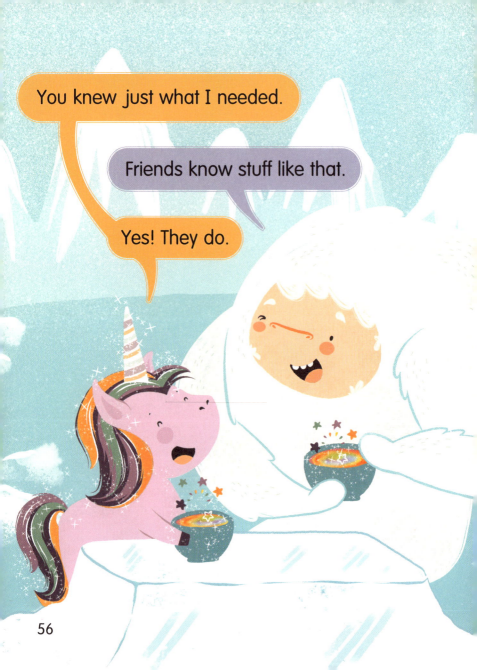

About the Creators

Heather Ayris Burnell lives in Washington state where she loves spending time in the sparkly snow. Sometimes she even has snowball fights with her friends! Heather is a librarian and the author of *Kick! Jump! Chop! The*

Adventures of the Ninjabread Man. Unicorn and Yeti is her first early reader series.

Hazel Quintanilla lives in Guatemala. Hazel always knew she wanted to be an artist. When she was a kid, she carried a pencil and a notebook everywhere.

Hazel illustrates children's books, magazines, and games! And she has a secret: Unicorn and Yeti remind Hazel of her sister and brother. Her siblings are silly, funny, and quirky — just like Unicorn and Yeti!

YOU CAN DRAW UNICORN!

1 Draw a circle. Attach a larger semicircle below that. Then draw a smaller circle that overlaps the semicircle.

2 Add a snout and four legs.

3 Add one ear. Draw the face.

4 Add the other ear, a mane, and a tail. Then draw the horn!

5 Draw the details. Add stripes to the magic horn!

6 Color in your drawing!

WHAT'S YOUR STORY?

Yeti wants to be fancy so Unicorn makes him a fancy hat. What fancy thing would **you** make for Yeti? What would Yeti do while wearing it? Write and draw your story!

scholastic.com/acorn